ONLY THE SHADOWS BREATHE

LAWRENCE GEORGE JAFFE

Lawrence George Jaffe

ISBN: 979-8-9890481-7-5

Dedicated to

This book, Only the Shadows Breath, is dedicated to those who seek the ultimate truth and live or die in the attempt. Many thanks to the detective noir and hard-boiled detective authors who taught me with their incredible words and storytelling abilities, especially Raymond Chandler, Dashiel Hammet, and James M. Cain. And one who I call friend, Harlan Coben.

Lawrence George Jaffe

Dedicated to:

This book, Only the Shadows Breath, is dedicated to those who seek the ultimate truth and live or die in the attempt. Many thanks to the detective noir and hard-boiled detective authors who taught me with their incredible words and storytelling abilities, especially Raymond Chandler, Dashiell Hammett and James M. Cain. And one who I call friend, Harlan Coben.

Table of Contents

Only the Shadows Breathe

Lawrence George Jaffe

Introduction

Can you write a hard-boiled detective story in poetry? I don't know – you tell me after you read *Only the Shadows Breathe*. Here's what noted author and aficionado of the mystery genre Harlan Coben has to say: *"Like all of Larry Jaffe's poetry, the words are tools to tell the story. He offers hope out of the morass we call life. ONLY THE SHADOWS BREATHE is a unique and heady blend of poetry and detective fiction – poetry noir if you will – and I loved it."*
I love love hard-boiled detectives and their characters. I was brought up, check that, I brought myself up with the likes of Dashiell Hammett and Sam Spade and Nick Charles and his lovely wife Nora, Raymond Chandler and Philip Marlowe, and James M. Cain. Before the hard-boiled noir took my attention, there was the ever-insightful Sherlock Holmes created by Arthur Conan Doyle. I must admit I never really cottoned on to Poe's Auguste Dupin, the progenitor of the genre. I want to tuck Walter Mosley and Easy Rawlins into this group although he came later in my chronology.
I was hooked on the seamier side of life that these literary heroes navigated. Lately, I tend to be reading a slew of British sleuths (try saying that three times). I love following up on the clues that make up life and not just the noir deaths of these detecting protagonists.
This is not a psychological thriller, there is no psychology involved. It is straight out good against the most diabolical evil ever encountered perhaps. I am introducing a new concept to a poetry book with the introduction of a narrator to each of the poems (more about that below).
Take a wild ride with me and my poet/private eye who goes by the name of Hatcher. It is diabolical in places and almost fun. After all, poets can live in the noir and wear the fedora of the gumshoe. . Poetry noir if you can imagine.
One final thought, consider listening to Lana Del Rey as the soundtrack to this book. Afterall, I listened to Lana while writing this book, so it is only appropriate to allow you the same privilege.

Lawrence G. Jaffe
August 2024

Acknowledgements

My life is a series of poems dotted upon a landscape of words. I have lived a very diversified life meeting and getting to know lots and lots of folks. Some have turned out to be friends with friendships that have endured time and stubbornness. But for the purposes of now I would simply like to acknowledge and appreciate my family who must put with me for this portion of eternity. They are my biggest fans daughters Amber, Willow and Megan, son Devon and my dearly loved wife Shelley. There have been as stated many friendships over the years but a couple stand out with regards to *Only The Shadows Breathe* and they include the romantic poet of the Internet and publisher of this book William F. DeVault and the illustrious detective fiction writer Harlan Coben who believed in my ability to create poetry noir. I also would like to acknowledge Mr. Gregory Reed who I always call Mr. Reed for believing in me and my creations. Thanks y'all (yes I can use the most southern term –" y'all" because I am from the south – South Bronx that is!)

Introducing the Narrator

Dear Gentle Reader. I would like to present you with the narrator of these poetic tales. I created the narrator to provide some continuity to the poetry as each piece provides a narrative and component to the overall story. The narrator is the storyteller and chronicler of the events between victims, predators and of course our beloved hero Hatcher – poet and private eye. Think of this volume of noir poetry in an old-time radio broadcast with the narrator explaining the goings on to the audience (you). The raconteur moves you through the story line keeping you moving along to the ultimate climax. The narrator's voice will appear in boxes as below.

> The Narrator Speaks
>
> How do you do? You may call me Mr. Baker and I will be your storyteller/narrator for this work by Mr. Jaffe. He has encouraged me to speak my mind as I take you through this series of events concerning the intrepid private eye cum poet Hatcher who is the key protagonist in this little adventure. I will try to be kind to the victims and objectively curl your toes as our predator comes into play. I will introduce you to the poems that are featured in this collection to maintain your interest and the fluidity of the compilation. I am told by Mr. Jaffe that you should think of this work like jazz, as the poetic riffs are instantaneous and subject to innovation. Should you have any complaints about this work, please take them up with Mr. Jaffe as I

am merely the behind-the-scenes storyteller of Only the Shadows Breathe!

So, sit back, relax your garments, and get ready to take a ride into the unseemly and vicious thoughts of our predator, the pleas of the victims and the gallantry and bravado of our hero. Despite my initial skepticism, it is an awfully good read.

Mr. Baker: This is the title poem introducing you to the collection. A simple ditty to take you to the heart of the land where Only the Shadows Breathe! The poems that follow help set the stage and create the scenario for a land that has lost all sense of morality.

Only the Shadows Breathe

Life is a lost tombstone
where only the shadows breathe
a quaint soiree lost in culture
without civilization to back it up

Here mendicants accelerate
their yearning
and mothers prostrate themselves
falling backwards on tuning forks
in annihilation of sin

A complex artifact vanishes
in this temple of disquiet
monks behave indecently
and rabble rousers show their faith
in this place where

Only the shadows breathe

Behind The Shadows

Behind the shadows
lies a rich darkness
deep thick and
pungently delightful
like cutting edge
chocolates
that seep between
your lips
and invigorate the soul

Behind the shadows
lies seduction
too sensual to be
conceived by mortality
like organic honey
licked from
from sensual
fingers

Lawrence George Jaffe

Let There Not Be Light

It is not the light
that creates shadows

It is the darkness
that declares itself
supreme and free

Shadows reach out
surrounding and sensual
beckoning the caller
to destiny

– Tread lightly into the impossible

This is not the house
of color or dreams
it is the ingredients
of nightmares

Walking Sunset Boulevard

Making my way down
what was once known
as the Strip Sunset Strip
casting my eyes
searching for evil
and neglect

The street is not respectful
of its inhabitants
morality can never endure
only the ruthless survive
even they have a tough time

Corners disappear into alleyways
lights fade to dark
and between these walls
lie the denizens of a city
too tired to be fucked up

Rational is suspended
in this place where
only the shadows breathe
a reminder to not get lost
as you will never be found

> Mr. Baker: There is something unnerving about the scent of blood that our predator dreams of and perhaps his imagination has roots in truth…this poem sets the stage and mentality of he who stays anonymous known only by the moniker Blood Thirst!

It Was the Smell of Blood

Blood is on the mountain
Blood is in the sea
Blood runs all over me

The blood – there was so much of it. It dripped from face to toes. I don't know where it came from. I did not seem to be wounded or hurt in any way – just soaked in red. It could have been body paint had it not had this rotten metallic odor. It was the smell of blood.

As I breathed in the shadows, my emotions saturated with blood sense. I knew whatever I had done was wrong. But I wanted more.

I had to have more.

Signed,
Blood Thirst

Only the Shadows Breathe

> Mr. Baker: Our predator moves out of the shadows thinking to himself as if no one would listen. Would they? The next two poems speak their mind about life and lust.

Predator

An assignment
such as this
requires loneliness
and opportunity

Never seek out the forlorn
they are apprehensive
and wary

Seek the buoyant
and forgiving
their empathy
is warming the gods

They betray reckless
with their arrogance
they go in sight unseen

They are prey without knowing
They are prey without believing

Watch them as they huddle
on street corners
pretending indifference
pretending to not be afraid

Go forth and mark them
with your scent

Let them see your eyes
and wonder what it would be like

Seduction is a many-layered cake
be the icing to tempt
be the aroma to arouse
be who they always dreamed you would be

Use those dreams to beguile
and loosen their chains

Use your nightmares to entice
them into the shadows

Oblivion 1

Let's not be trite
and call this the doorway
to doom
or some other such location

This is the place
where oblivion lies

A still life penetration
with more than
loss of blood
it requires the
loss of soul

There is no dignity
no half-blamed metaphor
this is the unreal
faced with the unreasonable

it will be as if you never existed
a place of darkness so sublime
you will shudder
because you will know

blind
in the dark
and in pain

This is a sojourn of evil
encouraging the vile
so strong and palpitating
and unconfrontable

Welcome to oblivion
a place that fails to exist
does not appear on any map

or globe

A universe of disgust
a place so formidable
that even the brave
pass it by

Look neither left nor right

Best not to look at all

> Mr. Baker: Our hero, a rising star himself, he fancies himself King of the Poetry underground and a fanatically superb detective of the private eye variety.

Hatcher Private Eye

My name is Hatcher
poetic tour de force
and gumshoe

I come by my handle
honestly
well sort of

Folks in the know
know me

You won't find me
in yellow pages
I am anything but yellow

I am not your stalking dick

I don't do bullshit assignments
no marital crap
no conjugal anything

I'm who you call when
you've got no one else

I am who you call
when only the shadows breathe

> Mr. Baker: Hatcher's first case was an impossible doozy. Some say it takes a twisted mind to solve a twisted case. Perhaps that is so. But it still remains, that no one could solve the case of the dead woman bicycling but a poet turned gumshoe by the name of Hatcher!

The case of the dead woman bicycling

Mystery surrounds us
how can a dead woman
ride a bicycle
corpses don't lie
it was not a bicycle
built for two
just your routine mountain bike
the color of cerulean blue
a so-called girls bike
without the bar
although it makes you wonder
why a boy would want a
so-called boy's bike
with a bar
that could injure tender bits
but that is all rhetoric
questions must be asked
as to how a girl
really a young woman
could be dead and still pedal
it seems impossible
an act of hypocrisy
that no one could solve

how could this dead woman
drive through traffic lights
get caught on CCTV
at various intersections
yet still be dead
Hatcher watching
the video frame by frame
had a so-called aha moment
as he watched for the 13th time
it seemed the dead woman
had a twin who did the pedaling
and swapped herself for the dead woman
who died from hands not unseen
fingerprints proved the action
and showed that the dead woman
was not resurrected
nor resumed living for a while
the dead woman was truly dead
and her twin sister
well let's just say
Hatcher saved the day
and brought justice for
the dead woman
who was not riding the bicycle after all
it was the sister of course

> Mr. Baker: Hatcher is not just seeing things,
> the pulpable evil strikes back.

Dark Haloes

Dark haloes
on these angels

What am I to think
at times like this

Am I the only one
that can see these
dark haloes

– see into the eyes
of their beholders
and reveal thoughts
never seen or heard

Who wears these
silent dark haloes
disguising their ambitions

Dark haloes
hiding intrigue and guile
Dark haloes
bridging smiles
with covert desires

Dark haloes of night
covering suspicions
where only shadows breathe

> Mr. Baker: Our predator thinks beyond the box, basking in the evil in which he resides. He cannot take back what has already been repeatedly said. And he is at war…

Seeking Shadows

I no longer
look for the sunshine

I seek shadows
and hide in the darkness

Is it shame that has
brought me to
such attitude

Shame for the crimes
of the committed

– the hate spread
throughout the world
is finally catching up
with me

I spread that hate
as communicable disease

Using mediums of destruction
bullets lined with hate
shot from guns
shattering hearts

Lawrence George Jaffe

Bombs derived from hate
dropped from planes
and drowned minds
in an infantile paralysis

I spread hate with the
same fashion that I made munitions
focused on toxins of greed
that eat mankind alive

I no longer struggle with
that conscience
it never existed
or so it seems

It did not start that way
one nightmare led to another
I had to cover tracks of error
and mistake that betrayed
my beatitude

I could no longer think straight
lines of insurgency
my surreptitious plans were
born to hate and genuflect
the genocide bred from
these farms of deceit

Who but a fool could
fight such forces that stem
from evil the devil's guide

I am mankind dying

He shouted
and the lonely listened
and the hungry listened
but those fed and fat hardly
moved from their
couches of insurrection

You cannot wage a revolution
from your living room

Lawrence George Jaffe

Hidden Shadows

I hide in shadows
you can barely see me

I want you to know
That I am there
That I am tender

Yet strong for your desires

I stay in the shadows
only you can hear me breathe

> Mr. Baker: At risk of making my presence too known, as the narrator I run the risk of being too there and depended upon, instead of the story carrying on by itself. But for the moment, I feel I must engage you to this fact. Murderers think of themselves being on a holy mission either for themselves or some long forgotten god that wishes to make their presence known. On with the show!

Holy Hit Men

The parlor as dark
as his brogue

Tiny elfin fires
burned rapidly
in branches of his mind

to be
or
not to be

was not his only question

He dared ask

why
what for

And received
communion

Before his
apparent death

Lawrence George Jaffe

I Was Not Born a Killer

I was not born a killer
it did not come naturally to me

I was not raised by wild folk who
wanted to make another
Hitler or Dillinger or Dahmer
or worse

I was raised by
a rather nice conservative couple
not a dangerous bone in their
lonely middle-class bodies

I was not raised to kill
enamored
with blood or the
subsequent lust arousal

I was not bitten by
some strange
foreign creature
creating vampiric
feelings in me

I was not
born
raised
or bitten to kill

I kill because
I like to kill
I kill because the
slicing of life pleases me

I kill because the
sight of blood intrigues me
delights me like nothing else

I kill up close and personal
with a blade of the finest
Japanese steel personally
sharpened by me for the task
literally at hand

I love to watch life ebb
to dissipate and disappear
and that is why I kill

I watch their eyes
as I quench my thirst

I watch their faces
as they realize at that one
truly fatal moment
how fatal it really is

I cut their throat
at such a precise angle
a new smile
forms mid neck

They drool blood
blood so hot
uttering soft moans
a deadly orgasm

The little death turned big

Lawrence George Jaffe

Interjection with a Promise

I feel I must speak up
you don’t know me
but I can already feel
your judgement calling
me out from the graveyard

I feel like I can tell
What you think of me
as you find yourself superior
because of my moral decline
or some such problems
with my lineage

Or you are crying for my
lost childhood
you don’t know me
you don’t know how
I arrived at this posture

How I tenderly dynamited
my previous life
only to land in this one
no you don’t know me

And you may only catch
a glimpse of my solidarity
how I have built up
a quiet resolution of me
one that you might find uninhibiting
and somewhat relaxing

– But it is too late for recrimination

It is too late for you
to make up some mumbo jumbo
about me and my motives

I could break out
Into song and dance
about Me and My Motives
and sing you songs
of political restraint

The lyrics would be deadly
and you would only
need to hear them once

> Mr. Baker: There is an undercurrent in this City of Angels. There is an underground market, and I don't mean the farmers variety. No, in this market, it is people, not produce being sold.

Black Honey

The river runs deep through our city

Historically worked hard

Travelers reveled in its wake

Commerce made its way

Slaves traversed in caravan

Suspicious cargo hustled into night

Black Honey
Black Honey
Black Honey

Forgotten Avenue

There is a street full of lonely dreams
She lives there

At the corner of Forgotten
And Unloved

I happened upon her accidentally
This girl child of broken promises

She hung out in alleys and gutters
Lived to no one's avail

But gutted out an arrangement
With the proctors that lined the streets

She sold herself as easily as she could coffee
And was a slave like her forbearers

No one could act less accordingly
No one could grasp her caldron

She was nowhere woman come to life

She bristles with thoughts

Of what could have been
And might be

She lives on Forgotten Avenue
And wishes she could forget

Lawrence George Jaffe

Something Is Wrong In the City

It was supposed to be the city of angels
now it feels like the city of devil spawn

Houseless on every boulevard
Smitten with ill-gotten desire

Children are sold
on every street corner

There is no wonder
It is not a conscious act

The mood is ridicule
The mood is silent offering

There is no penance
for those who seek redemption

They sit and wait in infamy
no turning of other cheeks

– here the lesser of two evils is death

> Mr. Baker: The predator reveals more of himself, speaking and withdrawing from the shadows so to speak. Beware if you are sensed by him.

Blood Sense

Blood is on the mountain
Blood is in the sea
Blood runs all over me

There is a sixth sense. It is a perception of hunters and birds of prey. They/we can sense a victim, our prey from miles off. It is not an inference that many have, but those who have this intuition will know what I am talking about. We smell the blood, but it is more than just a smell. It is a sense of the prey's desperation we scent and act accordingly. I will leave it to your imagination as to what act accordingly means.

Signed,
Blood Thirst

Lawrence George Jaffe

Blood Graffiti

The walls of
the men's room
were stricken with
graffiti

Your name written
in blood from
festered wounds
wounds left open
to heal
but decayed

The blood drips
in tight rivulets
pausing at the cracks
in the tiles
to once again drip
down the walls

Your name screams
from its purchase
no longer anonymous
your phone number
unrevealed
your name just meant
to tease not haunt

It still drips from the men's
room walls shouting your
indiscretions and your discredit

Only the Shadows Breathe

Our futile attempts
at immortalization
my last attempt
shouting from
the men's room
walls

Falling for the Dead

I Am Dead
He is death

I could no longer
wander in my dreams
his imagination
suffocated mine

I was dead
yet felt I could talk
if anyone would listen

I wanted to let the world know
of his existence
before he took someone else
on this one-way journey

But my tongue removed
by corporal nemesis
refused to wag

My lips could not form words
no matter how hard I tried
I could not speak another word

I was dead
and no one would listen to me
no one would listen to my warnings

No one could see me
I was transparent
and everyone could see
through me

I was dead
yet somehow still myself

How could this be
I wondered to myself

How could I be dead
yet still be alive

I hovered over this scenario
closed eyes that could not see
and sank into pleasant stupor
filled with imagination
and wonder

Despite death
I was still alive

> Mr. Baker: The wicked have a way of surviving unbeknownst to the populace at large. The wicked may sink to new depths but the victims, ah the victims
>
> find their resting place without grandeur.

And They Wind Up Dead

In this cemetery of fallen angels
lies one gentle soul after another

It is a place that has no history
A place where those laid to rest
have no past
and obviously no future

Once they are planted
in this garden
of eternal rest
they go on to their next journey
hopefully it won't have the same

Destination

> Mr. Baker: Our hero has been making noise and is being noticed by those who stay in the shadows.

Evil Rising

Evil rises at Hatcher's door
somehow
he has gotten wind
of the slaughter
on Los Angeles' beautiful streets
a place where no one goes to slumber
in fear of never waking up

> Mr. Baker: Evil is coming sooner than expected. Evil is always a surprise, especially to the naïve.

Evil Rising Loneliness Grips

loneliness grips
a double bladed
sword that wrenches
life askew there is no
handle only blood
dripping tenderly
from both hands

> Mr. Baker: Hatcher does not know when our predator will strike next. All he knows is that women, girls really, are being slaughtered by the handful and no one knows why, and no one seems to care, and Hatcher feels he must stick his nose or better, yet his gun filled hand and remove the predator from the land. In this somewhat innocuous setting our hero rants and rages.

Room for Rent

The sign hung precariously
yet respectfully
from the window
Room for Rent

Ads were run in the
local paper
Room for Rent

He even ran an ad
on the internet
Room for Rent

As I read this
totally innocuous
sign I got very angry
with the world
and especially at this landlord

For some weird reason
the sign in all of
its peacefulness
said life goes on…

while people die
and take drugs
and beat their wives
and lovers
and children are abused
and patients are drugged
instead of treated
as they go hungry

And I wanted to yell
at this unknown landlord

I wanted to shake
my fist in his face
grab him by the shoulders
and say something to him
something that might
just might wake him up

I wanted to tell him
I wanted to look him in the eye
and tell him
that while he was calmly
trying to rent his room
people were going hungry
and dying

Why was I ranting
at a homeless landlord
anyway

> Mr. Baker: Just an aside but the room for rent was rather cool.

Post Apocalyptic Fandango Apartment for Rent

it may be the end of the world passing
but a new age is rising
this apartment bears witness
that even survival can be funky

> Mr. Baker: Our predator teeters on his impossible dream. His soul captured by consequence. It is a long way to sanity, as if his victims lie inside him in anything but silent repose. Before his most desired kill, there was Angela.

Angela Is No More

Once upon a time
she shouted in fear
for her life

She shouted and shouted
and no one heard

This woman named for the angels
would never fly again

her blood splashed in heaven
in her guilty repose

A cut throat is more reprehensible
than a muddled mind

She sits on the trigger
that brought her down

But it was the knife
that did the most damage

A severed larynx could never talk
a blade she could never describe

A tattoo on her heart captured
the blood siphoned from her throat

Goodbye Angela fare well in heaven
or wherever you may go

She Did Not Go Quietly

I can still hear her screams
even though they were silent
they were impatient and brutal
my senses assaulted

She did not go quietly
My angel of the slums
she should have been happy
to be released from such squalor

She had to scream
and scream until my ears hurt
I can still hear her

i can still hear her screams
though her sliced throat
cut so finely from lobe to lobe

I can still hear her plea
to let her go but I could not relent
I could not let her go
There was nowhere to go

I could not let her run rampage
over my memories
allowed to think
she got away

I could not
let her run wild
her blood squirting
it would make such a mess

Only the Shadows Breathe

I silently closed her eyes
she could rest forever
no more screams
let out from her fragile body

No more screams assaulting my ears
she looked so pretty
sprawled on the tarmac
her hair a wild bush
her smile etched in memory

Body Count

Angela was just one of
how many more

Like logs tossed in a fire
her death was just another

In a countless battle with
he who thirsted for blood

How many more was unknown
and the populace ran scared

Especially young women of color
or lack thereof

Walking Away

With silent footsteps
mixed with trepidation
he staggers away
not turning his head
to look back to his latest
work without recrimination
just death on the tarmac

> Mr. Baker: it may have once been the city of angels but now it can only be classified as the city of diablo, the devil.

Walk On The Wild Side

The streets are narrow
and never empty
a bouquet of something rotten
permeates the airwaves.

It is as if life should never
have inhabited these fairways
life is combustible
and subject to whim

This is not just
a walk on the wild side
it's a place even Lou Reed
would not dare tread

These are streets of nightmares
avenues of disrespect
boulevards of hate
the street signs shout KEEP OUT

Our predator knows his way
around all the dark alleys
that hide between the streets
citizens beware

Hatcher also walks these streets
a constant reminder
that he was still a presence
in this godforsaken land

Lawrence George Jaffe

Hatcher Smells Blood

It was a day like no other
the sun barely shined
the wind was intolerable

The masters of the universe
seem to have gone on strike
there was a metallic smell in the air

the smell of blood wafted
through the universe
and unaware descended
in Hatcher's nostrils

his eyes were no longer cloudy
his expression no longer languid
he looked like a man on the scent

And he was
blood sent
blood scent

> Mr. Baker: It was one of those moments that made Hatcher hold his breath and turn his thoughts into a whisper. He felt like someone just walked over his tombstone.

Poet's Last Breath

The poet's last breath
was a poem
he liberated
from the past

It spoke of waves
and shenanigans

It spoke of doppelgängers
and repetition of lives

It spoke of war
and famine

as if they were
one drawn out
breath

the last one

Lawrence George Jaffe

> Mr. Baker: It is now time for a moment's repose. A place to rest your wits and listen to the dulcet tones of Lana's music. Hatcher needs a break too. Life can be very intense in the City of Angels.

Combustion

His feet dance
through life
one song at a time

Toe twitching rhythms
drinking notes
only he can hear

His feet expressing
themselves in
dance man tunes

His dreams
making soulful
energy force beats
that captivate
every thought

Dragging his torso
to and fro
his mind hanging
on every refrain

Every riff
barrels through
knuckles and into
his fingers
as they snap

As they snap the
night away

Combustion…

> Mr. Baker: A not so anonymous note circulates the massive Los Angeles underground. Has Hatcher been found out?

Who Does This Guy Think He Is?

Someone's nose is out of joint
and he keeps sticking it
where it don't belong
ya know what I mean

Not sure who he is
or what he wants
but he's getting
to be a nuisance

He's got to be taken care of
I don't mean buying
him a cup of coffee
and sending him on his way

I mean giving him
a bus ride with
a one-way ticket clutched
in his not so lively hand

Hot On the Trail

Tombstones are steppingstones
to another life one not so grand
it is called death

You don't want to follow
these footsteps through
the gates of a cemetery

You want to reverse tracks
turn around and run don't walk
the other way

Cemeteries may be picturesque
but they remain unsuitable
for picknicks or Saturday night dates

Hatcher was on a course
directly into the heart of evil
relentlessly he pressed on

Did he know what was aimed
at his pulsing heart
or was he just oblivious

to the rage that hunting him down

Lawrence George Jaffe

> Mr. Baker: Who says that killers don't have feelings? This predator performs his act as ritual and rites of love. Who is to say he is wrong – after all love conquers all or so they say.

Caressed By Shadows

It is not that I feel indecent
or even remotely withdrawn
I have become your worshipper

I dance with darkness
seeing everything
watching
hearing
sighing

My duress derived
from mental restraints
far more stringent than metal

Moral handcuffs chafe my wrists
immobilizing tactile states

I sit bathed in darkness
caressed by your shadows
your beautiful face
clothed in godless passion

I envy your skin
how it envelops you
hugs you with profound caress

I am at your mercy
yet feel no loss of control

Only the Shadows Breathe

I live in paradox
caught up in love
and distance

But admiration
lingers like delicate
baby breath caresses

I feel from you
with closed eyes

A solitary tear
strays from your left eye

> Mr. Baker: There is an unknown victim in all this clamor, a woman, a lady who through destiny had gained a status afforded only to a few. She rules her roost with velvet gloves and seems aloof to the circumstances that contain her betrayal. More to come…

The Lady Breaks

They called her Lady D
although she went by many names
Delores being the most prominent

– She was winsome and full of guile

when she swept into a room
she ruled it
every eye glued
to her countenance
and frame

The Lady caused
the most confident to stutter
the loudest to tranquil

You would think she could cure cancer
or malaria or any disease
with just her look
and perhaps a silent gesture

The almighty might bow down to her
such was her visage

But all that was yesterday
today she stood silent
withered with shame
her countenance a mere reflection
of her lore

Of course
she was not
who they thought her to be
but that was part of the mystique
her many nom deplumes
gave her introduction to societies
polite or not

Today a silent door had shuttered
her usual beauteous demeanor
lay shattered at her footsteps
now her clothes hung listlessly
from her tired frame

This was not the woman
many worshipped
This was not the woman
who wore tiaras at breakfast

Lady D
Lady Nothing

She needed help in the worst way
though she was yet to know it.

Who could she turn to
in her hours of distress?

Broken Hearted

Her heart has been broken
too many times
paralyzing her thoughts
and very beingness to the core

What becomes of the broken hearted
was more than just a song
it was a mantra she wore on her sleeve
a code of defiance to anyone approaching her

Have you ever seen a broken rainbow
this was her identifying with freedom riders
but never getting a foothold
on her true identity

It did not stop the blood thirsty
what could be more appetizing
than the blood
of the broken hearted

The Lady Needs You

On this October morn
when nothing relented
into something

She kept her visage
but underneath she was stricken

She would call on Hatcher
not to simply wash away the blues
but really to save her life

She was being stalked
and knew not why
or by who

She smiled at the mirror
the thought of Hatcher…

Lawrence George Jaffe

Deus ex Machina

She was the dove of uncertainty
falling uphill to a fading star
she sat in the shadow of shadows

looking
looking

Always searching
for something
barely or not there

She transformed miracles
into everyday attire
wearing them proudly

She did not know
what she knew
the root cause retribution

She was carried
over the threshold
into dawn

> Mr. Baker: He is a poet after all and a poet he shall always be.

Reading Schmeading

I'm at my favorite reading
at the old Moondog Café
on Melrose

All my friends and peeps are there
for my feature performance

I feel kinda blessed
and kinda hopeless at the same time
afterall poetry is like a lifeboat
in the stinking ocean

The Lady herself is there
how I miss her
now that's she's discarded me

But still there must be
some spark
since she just showed herself
into the back room
where the festivities
were just starting

I feel protective of her
and wonder how to get her back

Little did I know
that she came tonight
for professional service
not poetic ones

Post Reading Blues

After the reading
the Lady more than
anything wanted
to be held by Hatcher
and cling to his poetic self

She looked at him with salvation
on her mind
she clung to Hatcher in her wishes
but alas he was besieged by others
signing books and talking amongst his fans

He looked so poetically respectable
that she could not break that trance

She backed away from him
and the Moondog crowd
and sought solace in the night

Suddenly the wind whispered
her name and she felt someone
grab

The Lady screamed

Hatcher stunned
came running

Stop or I Will Shoot

The air hung heavy

My fingers lingered
on the pistol grip
a light feathery touch of fear
tendrils that made me
made me
want to take that thing

Pull it from its holster
Like the weapon it is
And
Bam
Bam
Bam
Anything in sight

I caressed the grip of Black Beauty
like a Saturday night lover

Gasping at the feel of Bakelite
it had no warmth
not endowed with any sense
it just could shoot bullets faster
straighter
more deadly than any before it

I wanted to draw that gun
more than life itself

I waited
Let the game come to me
Let it come

I would be ready

The Beauty in my holster
would be ready too

Only Shadows

Hatcher gun drawn
ready to do battle

The lady appeared
out of the mists

She appeared disheveled

Wanting nothing more
but Hatcher to hold her

They moved to each other
passion once forgotten
remembered

And held each other
for what seemed like forever

Lawrence George Jaffe

> Mr. Baker: Another grand moment to listen to the chanteuse while the poet moves to create an environment filled with… but our blood thirsty friend has other ideas.

Isle of Forgotten Dreams

Pseudo-monks line the avenue
like vultures on pedestals
searching for the near dead
for those who cannot quit their addiction
and those who dream of redemption

Sucking the soul from another
is not all that different
than drinking their blood
for those who lie
in contemplation and wait
with infinite patience
they seek their next quarry

Their wait is rewarded
in soulless siege
and revenge
another
and
another

> Mr. Baker: the blood thirsty vision is not what you might think…

Shadows Passing

Two shadows
Passing in the night
Too quaint
Only they didn't pass
They stopped
Mingled
And made love
Then the plunder

> Mr. Baker: And now for a brief poem to keep back the infidels of life.

Dust On The Rose

there is dust
on the rose
I gave you

it weeps silently in
a vase without water

I remember the
rose in deepest red
now it is tired shadow

when I took the rose
from behind
my smile
your dimples displayed
a pleasure half filled
with mirth
and desire

when delivered
they were fresh
with morning dew
today they sit lifeless
with dry tears

> Mr. Baker: Reality has a way of punching you in the mouth. Hatcher takes it like a man.

Ain't No City of Angels

This ain't no city of angels
no how no way
the only singing
we hear is devil's song

The preachers here
are all ex-alkies
they don't talk to god
and god don't talk to them
they listen with half
an ear anyway
so god couldn't get
two cents in anyhow

No this ain't no city of angels
it's a wicked place
where only the wicked
survive
and you have to be mighty wicked
ta even do that

I would tell ya more
but what's the use
you won't come round
here no more
so who cares
and good riddance
that's what I say

Lawrence George Jaffe

I gotta look out
for my own
and I got my hands
filled with that

That and a lot of dread
pent up dread
the kind that animals make
cuz we all be animals here

Even those who have converted
ain't no spirit left
and what we got left
is fool's fodder anyway

So don't be so self-righteous
when you be crossing
that street
don't think you are invulnerable
for one blasted minute
no sir

You got the willies just like me
Yeah
You got the willies just like me

> Mr. Baker: Another victim bows down to the so-called rectitude of life. A city is bewildered by what has transpired. Hatcher is filled with clues and death.

Tourist Trap

The tourist lay on the ground
all pretense of life gone

Someone had taken
a sledge to her lovely face

And beauty departed
with a wink and no nod

She was visiting
Grauman's Chinese Theater

With hope of after
dinner entertainment

She lies there
recumbent

With no hope
or reservation

For a dinner
she never had

Her face lethal
in recumbence

The smile nonexistence
sadness pervades the routine

Her friend barely shock recovered
He came out of nowhere

There's a killer on the loose
and he's not done

Stolen Lace

The past was not an accident
angry tendrils of shadow
intervened

Evidence of evil lurked
disturbing bystanders
who could not see

It's only a shadow
they thought
as blackness descended

The crepuscule never abandoned
starlight attempted
to right the scene

Only darkness matters
faint whispering giggles
could be heard

A fine piece
of lace was stolen
and never traced

it was found around
the neck of the next
victim

An emotion of negligence
was detected
just a scrap of lace

Was it a clue

Feed the Shadow

A poet wonders if he will ever get lucky
He wrote the poem
gave her his best shot
but now he looks as though
he has run out of luck

He was told
he must
feed the
shadow to survive

No one told him
the shadow
was not his own

> Mr. Baker: Hatcher calls upon the shadows to release the predator.

Boxing Shadows

At the corner of my right eye
lurks a monster
of mammoth proportions

He appears
and reappears
when least expected

He transforms himself into a miracle
calls out the bastions of faith
walks away indifferently
disappears into the seams of fate

This is my nemesis
my calling
he is hideous yet beautiful
a creature of dichotomy

He lives within
he lives without
his destination and purpose
beyond simplicity of me

I stretch out my arms to him
this hidden father
and lapse into prayer
gibberish springing from my lips

Like sodden gun powder
Fearing I will explode at any moment
Fearing that I will not explode

Lawrence George Jaffe

> Mr. Baker: How do I love thee, let me count…Nah! Forget about it.

Waiting by the Mirror

I stand looking at the mirror
observing the shadow
cast by your reflection.

I wait alone
the sun has stopped shining
yet there is still shadow.

I do not understand the loneliness
that beckons from distant
street corners.

A woman with cigarette
dangling from rubied lips
asks me if I want to dance.

I stumble across her feet.

I don't smoke I say.

She looks at me disdainfully.

I wonder what treachery
has been crossed as
I stand by the mirror waiting
hoping to see your
reflection in my eyes.

Blank stares
and personas beware
are what I discover.

Only the Shadows Breathe

The phone does not ring
despite hopes of pregnant pauses
or relevant moments together
sharing coffeehouse eclairs
something sweet that
does not wither the soul.

I wait feverishly by the mirror
hoping against hope you
will rescue me from my demise
from winsome strangers
wooing my heart.

I await miracles
seriously considering
converting to any religion
claiming my heart.

My neck so weighed down
by crucifixes and stars and
trinkets from unnamed gods
I can no longer lift my head.

I kneel by the mirror
waiting slowly waiting.

Lawrence George Jaffe

> Mr. Baker: The predator moves on and on and on, energized by the bloodlines of the city.

She Felt the Horror

Before she saw the wicked
little carving knife
she felt such horror

Immobile with fear
she watched it
move tenderly to her throat

She could not move
and awaited the pain
the sudden rush of empty

But funny thing happened
on the way to death
it didn't happen

Her courier of bad news
murmured wrong one
and ran off

She sat on the alley ground
recited several Hail Mary's
and fainted

She came to with
a paramedic
giving her oxygen

She did not know how lucky
she was

But then she started to scream
and scream and scream

And…

Bloodlines

Blood is on the mountain
Blood is in the sea
Blood runs all over me

Someone joked metaphorically that I had blood on my hands. Little did they know. My hands, my fingers my feet, my toes. From top to bottom I was soaked in blood. So, I took a shower and watched all that delicious blood go down the drain. Whose blood was it you may wonder and ask. Nobody really. No one you know. Just someone from the neighborhood who rented a room down the street.

Signed,
Blood Thirst

I Am Shadow

I am shadow
that dangerous vortex
from which evil spills
its malicious binds

I am shadow
malevolence Raised
to the highest levels
sucking the life from you

I am shadow
a breeding ground
for horror and dread
I can hide anywhere

I am shadow

> Mr. Baker: A lady whistles and wonders
> what has she begotten?

Shadow player

I live in the shadows
my eyes seek access
to your fate
to scourge or joy

I remain indifferent
a teleprompter of destiny
sharing pleasure or pain

My will propels me
in congested direction
sometimes hands flail
a compass gone amuck

I pledge allegiance
to ignorant flags
and once burned my books
to censor my thoughts

Life proves to be cruel legislation
the handbook printed
on disposable tissue
a puff pastry of instant gratification

I make these shadows my home
camouflaged negligence

No one can see my cowardice
No one can feel my pain
No one can see my beauty
No one can see my courage

But it is your future we discuss
not my calumny of life

My fickle fingers pointing away
and now I pretend to watch you closely
it has all become pretense

Who has the tightest glare
Who can see through the stars
Who can shape the universe

With un-translated fingers
I wander through your spiritual incest
wondering why there is no guide
your mind closed cipher

The sun neither rises nor sets
The moon a jaded widow

This is truly a noble profession
I think to myself ironically
dwelling in my self-imposed stockade
suffering from knee-jerk sentimentality

I pack my bags for transfer
to a less prestigious abode

You need not say another word
grace your final chapter
written in fury and flame
violence never your stock and trade
you took it up as past time

They thought no one would cross the barrier
What makes you think I did not
I push you past defenses
of your own creation

Lawrence George Jaffe

No maternal
No material
Needs granted

You carry out your clown filled destiny
singing utterance
with misplaced growl

A cowgirl preoccupied with life
will you ever take flight
or forever be haunted
by your own fears

Will you ever accept self
as divinity

How many turns must you take
before you finally reach the beginning
your Mesopotamia

Your catalog of dreams
no longer one-dimensional
black and white

With tear dripping beneath right eye
for things lost
golden moments of triumph
separated forever
your heart cries in melancholy translation

Then you sit stone-faced
drawing a new sentence
on the fragile leaves of life

You hope for rum cake to ease
the pains of struggle and indifference
you receive jailer's bait
tell your story from stem to stern
languish in your own nirvana

And like the wind
you whistle
And like the wind
you are fierce

But winds die down
and you are left alone
with stormed tears

Your clever moves archetyped
in seething soliloquy
roundly attacking oppressors
willingness left unscathed

Is it true
that you are the most beautiful
woman in the world

As hearts are laid to rest at every juncture
your winsome loveliness worn like shackles
did it take a man to move the flames asunder

You listen to the words of an indifferent god
who has abandoned his creation
Even though
there is no one prouder at sunrise
than him

But it takes a real god to deal with sunset
and darkness

Lawrence George Jaffe

This god is not Houdini and he cannot
erase it with foul sweeps of hand
as if magic could make it go away
as if magic could make it better

He glorifies his own words
He lives in a rash of his own religious fervor

His sleeves sprout cufflinks
In macho godly challenge

Staking his claim in eternity
shooting down predecessor
ne'er-do-well
and pretender to idyllic chambers

He still listens to your prayers
He waits for you to worship him

I cannot
I don't want anyone to die for my sins
I find myself newly filled with hope
and dreams

But it is freedom I finally seek
Icarus wings await me

They may not be what I need
but I must move on
to waken to another dawn

I would eat monk's bread for breakfast
and pronounce
It is not a dream to be alive
It is not a dream

Blade Light

at the
very tip of the blade
at the point
at its edge
lies a darkness
of penetration
here the light
refuses to reflect
here is the
point of entry
to doctored souls
relieved of worldly
possessions
at knife point
testifying injustice
when only
a bloody rag
will do.

Lawrence George Jaffe

> Mr. Baker: Hatcher worships from afar contemplating his loss and the shadow's gain.

Odd Beauty

As the shadow
of moon curved
into your cheekbones
I was curiously overtaken
by your beauty
rising from forces
nontraditional

The moon seemed to call out
highlight
enlighten
refocus
the struggle of your sorrows
and how you mastered them
reforming them
into beauty
not pain

I watched carefully
this curious metamorphosis
as planets realigned themselves
in your eyes

As brows unfurrowed
and smiles overcame the
shadowed unhappiness
as you merged with life
from the crevices of angst

Only the Shadows Breathe

You smiled as you see me
and I wonder how
I can bring you
bring anyone
someone
so much joy

When sadness lies hidden
in my waxen features
and I wonder at your beauty
when my features
are bloated with emotions
less sought out than love
but your smile
seems to stretch
from lips of pure ecstasy
onto my own

I could never betray
such promise
with my own torch of sympathy

Do we dare contemplate
what does not exist

Do we rush where even
fools don't dare

Do you lead into decadence
or divine revelation

Your eyes sing love songs
my ears cry in repose
your memories never routine

And now you want my smiles
to cover the sounds of hearts
beating in acrid loneliness

Killer Sings

A killer hums and sings as he sharpens his knives.
What will you do
When he turns out the light
What will you do
When he shuts down the night
What will you do
When he turns into fright
What will you do
When holds you tight
What will you do
When you have lost the fight

> Mr. Baker: And now for a brief poem
> to alert you to the shadows and what
> or is it who stands behind them.

Soft Shadows

the soft shadows
of moonlight
cast my love on
your features
like a second skin
your smile beckons
in the distance
and you sigh
with misadventure
as our fingers rise
to touch

Dead Silence

On a wind-blown street
there are no lights
no water
no friends

The wind stirs up images
a swirling daughter of ghosts

Children play without toys
couples hold hands in the park
a woman shops
a man fixes a car
yet no one stands

Only their specter
shadows from a moon
darkened by war

A landscape of frost
delivers a hushed breathless night
and always the silent screams
the quiet deadly silence

Weapons cannot
pull their own triggers
they never seek retribution
war is silent
disapproving by nature

Is not the first quake of war
the greatest infidelity
brandishing swords
of disfavor

Only the Shadows Breathe

A man a woman a child
fall in a war
and no one hears them
are they still dead

Despite the sound
of weapons
the aggressor always
self-righteous
in the deliverance
of destruction

As the world remains quiet
couched in fear
hiding with muffled minds
does not the soul
rebel to the affliction of pain
upon another

> Mr. Baker: He thought life would move on, instead it seemed to go backwards neither staying the same nor giving him hope. Hatcher feels the loss of life as if an old friend had died. Which in a way just might be true. Lady D has disappeared.

Gone

Where Did She Go
I looked everywhere
there was no here

She was
gone without the wind
to trail her

She disappeared
on a street of loveliness
as if she was never here

Oblivion strikes twice
once for life
twice for soul

She exuded rapid fortune
underneath an overlay
of innocence

And then with the snap of fingers
she was gone
everywhere was nowhere

Everything about her
was consumed
by shadows

> Mr. Baker: Even the predator feels as if something must happen, there must be some action to call his attention, otherwise he has failed in his mission.

Temptation's Bliss

He suffered from
temptation's bliss
he slithered
he did not walk

He moved with
shadowed disrespect
a fading personality
a ragged frame
folding and enfolding
from block
to block
street to
street
seeking solace
from the soulless

He moved
like a snake
slithering
unloved
unliked
unhated
not even disliked
he was completely nonexistent
in a town of passions
that passed him by

What kind of
man exists
like this so
non-extant
how could someone
not exist
yet he did for
he slithered
and did not walk

Oblivion 2

I walked into oblivion
without a map
a wave
or my sunglasses

I just walked
without running
did not want
to chance a ticket as
I had no license
to kill

No registration
or even oblivion insurance
for that matter

So I walked
did not speed my way
to oblivion

I walked
slowly
carefully
drinking my
forgetfulness
with every step

Psycho Love

It is not what
psychos want
that makes them
dangerous

It's what they think
they want
that makes them killers

They see a cop go by
and it is not hate
the psycho feels
he actually
feels love for
the policeman
the gendarme

He longs for their contact
their connection
the close tight touch
of that copper jacketed
slug meeting and
shattering breastbones

He dreams with passion
of the loving damage
he could cause on those
blue cased bodies

He pledges his heart
to the soul of lead
a maelstrom only requited
by death
his
others
it matters not
to the psycho
no one is truly alive

> Mr. Baker: The shadows speak and harken. Will no one listen to the plaintive tone? Will Hatcher discover his mistress of desire or will it forever pray on his conscience.

Oppression's Shadow

If you look closely
at every gentle being
and even the ones
supposedly fierce
you will see a shadow
crossing their face
It masks their features
closes their eyes
and deforms expression

It is the shadow of
oppression and
everyone wears it

Behind their smiles
and lies
lives the shadow

But I no longer am
desirous of carrying this
yoke of slavery and
suppression

Only the Shadows Breathe

I will no longer wear
the shadow of oppression
on my furrowed brow
nor drink from the trough
of deception

You can no longer imprison me
with your own inadequacy
nor lock me in chains
of deceit

I am a slave no more
I wear the yoke
and shackles no more

And you may wield
your impotence
like a magic wand but
its flagging spirit can never
imprison
anyone
again

> Mr. Baker: Little does our hero know, but life is on the line not just his but his one true love might never see the light of another day. And poetry I just might lay forgotten at the shadow's door.

Betsy Barks

I'm no stranger
to danger

But sometimes
you just have to weep
because your heart
is thinking better
than your mind

And you are just
up to close
to see the big picture

When I have to wave
Betsy around to attract
someone's attention
it usually means my
gig has gone awry far awry

So this is what happened
that Christmas Eve
when I was spending
too much time with friends
aka my mug of brew

Only the Shadows Breathe

Like most Christmas Eves
I was alone
my whole life
is about being alone

My pillow is my mistress
check that
Betsy
my sweet Glock
is the only friend I have

Now that does not mean
I am lonely or nothin
it just means I spend
a bit too much time
with my shooter

And not with some dame
Okay not just any dame

There is a woman in my life
and I see her when I can
she goes by the name of Delores
and she is mighty special to me

But I don't want her
to get too close
on account of my profession
if you know what I mean

And she won't succumb
to passion's door
without provocation

Delores and me go way back
and I want her to have a good life

Not tucked up with a lout like me

Yeah Yeah
I may be poetic but that's
a long way from romantic
if you know what I mean

So like I said me and Delores
go way back
and I was feelin a might nostalgic
there was a midnight poetry reading
I wanted to take her to

The sentimental side
had got her a little gift
and I wrapped it up
all nice

And what could it hurt
If I went to see her
She might not be alone
I thought to myself

But then again
she might be
and what the heck
did I have to lose
she loves the Christmas poetry read

So I decided to hoof
it over there
when I saw something
in the darkness

It was like a shadow
wriggling in the moonlight

I was all set to say
it was my imagination

But then I saw the glint
off the pistola aimed my way
quicker than you could
say Humphrey Bogart

Betsy was in my hand and barking
like the good girl she was
I hear a thud and a slight murmur
Betsy had done her job

And it looked like
I would not be seeing Delores
or reading poetry
that night

Which was kinda sad
If ya knows what I mean

> Mr. Baker: And so my friends this journey with semi-happy ending draws to a close. thank you for listening to my plaintive words and may you think of Hatcher and Lady D as thus…

Never to Leave You Alone

There is no admiration here
only hallucinatory tears
ripping the canvas away

You once struck me as friend
but now I see your game plan
and am revolted by your passion

My blood lies belittled
a puddle of your frustration

I have wilted like the flower
I never was

I am your crucible
and your crucifix

You leave me apparently whole
yet castrated

I play act as your puppet
but now am just lifeless form

Who kidded who
Who leaned on the gas pedal
to oblivion

I am your Kama Sutra
I am your Dharma
I am the Bardo Thodol
Your Tibetan Book of the Dead

I remain unborn
to haunt your dreams
caress your desires
and prevent your redemption

I am your Karma

You will be beseeched
You will not remain unblemished

Your cause is my cause
We are alike
We are one

Your death is on your hands
your principles scattered

I am a perpetual hello

Never to leave you alone

Never to leave you alone

Filigree of Pain

From the depths
of the human cesspool
to the bright lights of
Broadway exploiting pain
and grief with
soliloquies and diatribes
and moving pictures
of soiled memories

Usurping lives taking over
mental processes with
enforced recollections
of degradation
shrinking spiritual
beings to bodies

Can you feel the pain
projected from the soul

Can you drink the potion
the draught of hate
that filters through
lives yet still smile

Weighed down by
this sea of chains
encrusted with
past passions
hates and deeds

Holding populace in place
infected with mental leprosy
losing minds and thoughts

Society's foothold
treading in this swirling chaos
and backwaters of a
mass of public indignation
disguising the truth
misdirecting the points
of it all

Can you hear the cries of
freedom lodge in throats
of a populace that never yields

from deep within the tomb

A silent shadow trembles
with caressed desperation
of an aphrodisiac
and smiles oft riddled with pain
anonymous tortures remembered and
the slaves' shackles soon dismembered
by last ounces of will and salvation

A being on spiritual pilgrimage
the glory knows no bounds

Can you see society wince
at this presence
as they overcome the despair

Opening shattered hearts
reaching deeply to this
latticework of pain
tears paying penitence
exhuming every facet

Every shard of agony
gathering strength from trust
sliding this spiritual sword
from the embers
like Excalibur from stone

Slicing through the ravages of time
that holds this prison eternal
praying for hope and peace
and then drinking tribute
to a cause no longer lost

This filigree of pain
carefully shows off
its anguished facets holding
forth the enemy to eyes
lost with emotion
and tears refusing to cry

Pain is held in heartbeats
a burning crescendo
of breathless illusion

We beseech gods
looking down from
Olympus testing our mettle

And man has dared to pass the test
this poem is a death
sentence commuted

Encouraging the hope
blowing against the ember

Only the shadows breathe

Cops Come a Calling

My night of poetics
turned into poetry noir
Betsy had done her job
now it was my turn
to belly up to the bar of life

I looked down to see
Betsy's handiwork
It was a jamoke
I had seen before
but didn't really know

He was a clown named Morgan
who wanted to make a name
for himself
and make me a notch
on his belt once he had his fun
with Lady D

I was the cavalry saving
the damsel in distress
but the officials might have
a different story

Cops came to discover
the ruckus
took Betsy for tests
and me for disturbing
the peace

Morgan was shuttled
to the morgue
the less said the better
but the detectives
on the case knew me
and knew it was a righteous kill

All in a day's work
I said to myself

All in a day's work

The Shadows Still Breathe

Guns are fired lives are lost
But this is not the end
More criminals are hatched
Than return to the grave
There is always more drama
And Hatcher will need his trusty
pistola
More times than he would like

Why
Because only the shadows breathe

About the author

From the sensually romantic to humor and social commentary, Jaffe impacts audiences with a rich emotional range, masterfully crafted. His poetry appears in numerous anthologies, magazines, and on the Internet where he has pioneered poetry web sites. Jaffe claims to have been born on a mountaintop in the South Bronx, in the shadow of Yankee Stadium. From the time he could walk, he either was going to play baseball, hoops or be a poet. Sometimes he thought he was the spiritual reincarnation of Davy Crockett. He felt he had that mountaintop thing in common with Crockett. His folks once bought him a coonskin cap which stimulated this peculiar tangent. In truth, he is the product of his own dreams. And has fond hopes of being classified a world citizen walking in the shadows of Mr. Neruda. As for how he writes, Jaffe was once quoted saying that "The air is made of letters, I breathe them in and simply breathe out poetry." He writes with romance and a satirical tongue pressed firmly to his cheek. But do not take his sense of humor for lack of worldly concern.

For his entire professional career, Larry Jaffe has been using his art to promote human rights. He is a distinguished poet with tremendous following who prides himself on his community involvement and care. He was Poet-In-Residence at the Autry Museum, a featured poet in Chrysler's Spirit in the Words poetry program, co-founder of Poets for Peace, helped spearhead the United Nations Dialogue among Civilizations through Poetry project, Pushcart Nominee, and the recipient of the Saint Hill Art Festival's Lifetime of Creativity Award, along with other awards.

Lawrence George Jaffe

Jaffe has been featured in poetry venues and festivals both throughout the U.S. and abroad. He has read his work in such distinguished locations as the Japanese American Museum, Hammer Museum, the Jewish Museum and the Museum of Literature in Prague and the Dylan Thomas Centre in Wales. He loves to read in a variety of bookstores, coffeehouses, and bars to keep his roots intact. Jaffe's dynamic work integrates a strong sense of humor along with his tough stand on human rights and freedom.

He has six books of poetry: *Unprotected Poetry, Anguish of the Blacksmith's Forge, One Child Sold, In Plain View, 30 Aught 4, Sirens* and *Man without Borders, Abolitionist Poetry Handbook on Human Trafficking.*

He is not a newcomer to mystery noir fancying himself to be an undeclared love child of Raymond Chandler or Dash Hammett, or…

www.ingramcontent.com/pod-product-compliance
Lightning Source LLC
Chambersburg PA
CBHW010139030826
48979CB00023B/1045

9798989048175